POO ON MY SHOE

Patrick MacIsaac
&
Glen Crusoe

Illustrated by
Larisa Campbell

Illustrations by
Larisa Campbell

Other Books by
MacIsaac & Crusoe

The Frog that Crossed the Street

Archibald Goes to the Big Game

The Black Marsh Monster

Ghost Surfer

Lycosidae

I grabbed my school bag
And hurried out of the house,
When all of a sudden,
I smelled a dead mouse.
I walked faster and faster
To leave the horrible stink.
But it followed me close,
I didn't know what to think.

I looked left and right,
Then up in the air.
Then behind me, around me,
Then down, and then there...
There for all to see...
Every him, her, they, or who...
Right there!
There was POO ON MY SHOE!

Mr. Frank, the bus driver,
Held his nose and said, "Whew!"
I said, "What can I do?
It's poo on my shoe."
"That's really nasty,
And I'm sorry," said Frank.
"But you'd cause a fuss on the bus
With you smelling so rank."

My best friend Joey
hollered out from the bus,
"What'cha gonna
Do now, Stinky Gus?
I'd find a nice patch of grass,
If I were you,
And wipe away
That poo on your shoe."

In a spot of green,
My shoe got a scrub,
I wiped it and wiped it,
Then gave it rub.
But no matter how hard
I'd give it a try,
It was too late…
The Poo was all dry.

I was thinking ahead,
Sweating out apprehension,
Knowing the foul stench would
Get the whole school's attention.
And so I shuffled along…
Not moving too quick…
When in the school yard
I spied a dog pawing a stick.

"Here doggy, here doggy!"
I called, and then whistled.
As my new pal came close,
His nose twitched and sniffled.
I took the stick from his mouth
To poke the hard goo.
Still… it wouldn't let loose…
That poo on my shoe.

Rover, that was the name on his tag,
Saw that I was in need.
He wagged his tail, licked my nose,
And then promptly peed.
I couldn't believe it; he soaked
My foot through and through,
And softened and washed-off
That poo on my shoe!

Now my foot is all squishy,
And I walk with a squeak,
And I leave a wet footprint...
But at least I don't reek.
It just goes to show
A bad start can have a good end,
And to top it off,
I made a good friend!

DEDICATION

Thanks to all our family and friends.

And to all of those who came before us

for showing us the way.

ACKNOWLEDGMENTS

Thanks to:

Larisa Campbell, our excellent Artist,

To RL Stein and his Master Class writing lessons,

Patrick MacIsaac, author
I'm a willing traveler through the collective consciousness
of the universe, spinning tales and fables from dimension
and realms typically only traveled by the immortals.

Glen Crusoe, author
I have never grown up, not really. I watch butterflies and
birds and rabbits, and dogs and cats; all still put a smile
on my face. I enjoy stormy weather, and the quiet of still water.
Yet, I wonder, "What moves around beneath in the dark?

Larisa Campbell, illustrator
A native of Maryland, now living in Mississippi.
A mom, freelance artist, and crafter, when Larisa isn't
working on one of her projects, you can find her out in the woods
chasing squirrels and looking under rocks to add to her
rather impressive collection of wiggly little invertebrates.
https://www.instagram.com/l.campbell.art/

YOUR FREE BOOK IS WAITING AT

https://macisaaccrusoebooks.com/

GET IT NOW!

Author Contact: MacIsaac.Crusoe@gmail.com

Made in the USA
Middletown, DE
27 December 2021

57134888R00015